W9-AXZ-090

DISCARDED
from the Nashville Public Library

NASHVILLE PUBLIC LIBRARY

The Tortoise and the Hare Race Again

by
Dan Bernstein

illustrated by
Andrew Glass

Holiday House / New York

To Candia, the unlaziest rabbit I know

D. B.

For Rosie

A. G.

Text copyright © 2006 by Dan Bernstein
Illustrations copyright © 2006 by Andrew Glass
All Rights Reserved
Printed in the United States of America
The text typeface is Kosmik Plain.
The artwork was created in colored pencil with transparent and opaque watercolors.
www.holidayhouse.com
First Edition
1 3 5 7 9 10 8 6 4 2

Library of Congress Cataloging-in-Publication Data
Bernstein, Dan.
The tortoise and the hare race again / by Dan Bernstein ; illustrated by Andrew Glass.—1st ed.
p. cm.
Summary: Tired of being a celebrity, the tortoise challenges the hare to race again,
this time with the intention of losing.
ISBN-10: 0-8234-1867-7 (hardcover)
ISBN-13: 978-0-8234-1867-1 (hardcover)
[1. Hares—Fiction. 2. Turtles—Fiction. 3. Racing—Fiction.] I. Glass, Andrew, 1949– ill. II. Title.
PZ7.B4565Tot 2006
[E]—dc22
2005046373

It was another bad-hare day.

"You'll never guess who laughed at me *today*!" whined the hare to his mother. "The big fat Easter Bunny just stood there laughing his ears off!"

"Wouldn't *you* laugh at a hare who lost a race to a tortoise?" she asked.

"I came in *second*," pouted the hare. "That counts for *something*!"

Alas, it counted for nothing. The hare was a loser. The slow-and-steady tortoise caught the speedy little hare, mainly because the speedy little hare fell asleep on the homestretch. The hare woke up and then tried to *catch* up; but, as most people know, the tortoise won The Great Race. By a hair.

Ever since, not one rabbit had a nice thing to say to the hare. Not Pete R. Rabbit, not Warren Rabbit, not Rabbit Foote, the luckiest rabbit the hapless hare had ever met. Even Hare E. Plodder, the oldest, slowest rabbit in the village, believed *he* could have won The Great Race.

Whenever the lazy hare appeared, Stu Rabbit got boiling mad. Jack Rabbit ran circles around him. The White Rabbit dashed down the nearest hole. General Rabbit E. Lee marched his floppy rabbiteers in the opposite direction.

"If only I could race the tortoise again," moaned the hare to his mother. "Why, I'd clean his clock!"

His mother sighed. "You'd probably take another nap, dear."

The tortoise—Mr. Slow and Steady himself—wanted to race again too. At first the tortoise just loved being famous. He ranked No. 1 on the list of Most Admired Reptiles, barely beating out a creepy crocodile. He even wrote a best-selling book: *My Hare-Racing Experience*. Yet the tortoise soon discovered that winning The Great Race wasn't that great.

Take parades. He *hated* them.

"The average turtle parade lasts six weeks," the tortoise complained. "Guess who has to smile the *whole* time?"

He didn't like young turtles either. They always tried to race him.

"They must be nuts!" said the World's Fastest Tortoise. "If I lose, I'll be the only tortoise who beat a hare—and lost to a turtle."

The tortoise wanted the one thing his victory could not give him: a normal life of sleeping long hours, slurping juicy worms, and working at the shell station, shining turtles' backs.

It was only a matter of time before the tortoise and the hare planned a rematch.

"We'll start the race at sunrise," the tortoise announced.

But the floppy-eared fuzzball stretched and yawned.

"I'm not a morning hare," he said. "I'm not even an afternoon hare."

"I'll tell you what you are." The tortoise scowled. "You're a deadbeat, *lazy* hare.

That's what got us into this mess in the first place!"

"If I win," said the hare, "you have to buy me a pair of silk pajamas. I look terrific in purple."

"Fine," said the tortoise. "But if I win, you buy *me* some cool sunglasses." The tortoise thought sunglasses would allow him to hide. He had heard this worked in Hollywood.

The tortoise and the hare agreed to race the next day at noon. Turtles and rabbits from all over the countryside turned out for The Great Race II. The tortoise plodded to the starting line wearing a small yellow backpack.

The hare dashed up to the starting line wearing a large necklace of alarm clocks. Big clocks, little clocks, and even one cuckoo clock.

"No nap today!" declared the hare. "I'm going to be the hero of all the hares, the toast of all the rabbits!"

"Rabbits on toast! Rabbits on toast!" chanted the teenaged turtles.

Exactly at noon, a chorus of turtles and rabbits shouted, "Ready, set, GO!"
The hare bolted into the lead while the tortoise just put one foot in front of the other. It was hard to imagine how the hare had ever lost the first race.

"I can't even *see* the tortoise," panted the hare, who hadn't stopped running for an hour. "He's so slow he must be going *backward*. I get sleepy just thinking about it. Maybe I'll rest my eyes."

He crept behind a large rock, where a big brass bed with fluffy pillows awaited him. (Naturally, this was his own harebrained idea.) The hare fell asleep, but every alarm on his necklace was set. There was no way he could snooze and lose.

Meanwhile, the tortoise plodded forward, slow and steady. Even though he was far behind, the tortoise couldn't help worrying about the hare. I sure hope those alarm clocks work, he thought.

At that very moment, the alarm-clock necklace sounded bells, buzzers, bongs, beeps, chirps, chimes, and cuckoos.

The hare was so worried that the tortoise had passed him that he threw off his necklace and ran toward the finish line faster than he had ever run in his life.

Two hours later the plodding tortoise spotted a hare ball curled up and snoozing under a tree. The finish line was in sight!
"*Oh, no!*" groaned the tortoise. "Not again!"

The tortoise slipped off the yellow backpack and pulled out his secret weapon: It had two ears, two eyes, two very large teeth, one nose, four feet, and *tons* of fuzz. Hidden beneath a cotton puff was a powerful, 5,000-tortoise-power engine.

Yes, his secret weapon looked exactly like the hare.

With the sun setting and the hare snoring, the tortoise gently squeezed the right ear of his rabbit suit and the 5,000-tortoise-power engine roared to life. The tortoise zoomed across the finish line to the wild cheers of thousands of real, live, greatly relieved hares.

The tortoise flashed a victory salute, then squeezed his right ear again and zoomed away before the happy hares could get too close.

Deep in the forest, the tortoise crammed the rabbit suit into his backpack and plodded home. The next morning, at Turtle Town Square, turtles and tortoises actually seemed tickled with what the tortoise had done.

"You beat the hare once," said an old turtle with a wrinkly, crinkly neck. "None of *US* could do that!"

The tortoise was thrilled.
He felt normal again, plodding
forward, slow and steady,
as happy and content as a
retired racing tortoise could
hope to be.

The hare, who had slept until noon the next day, could not actually remember *winning* the race. But so many rabbits had congratulated him that even his own mother believed he had finally cleaned the tortoise's clock.

That morning a package arrived for him. He looked positively dashing in his new purple silk lounging pajamas. "I can't tell you how tired I am of this 'slow and steady' business," the hare said. "You know what won this race? Speed, baby. That wasn't just a hare they saw out there. That was a *machine*!"

The hare never
found out how right
he was.